CLASSIC
GRAPHIC FICTION

DR. JEKYLL
AND MR. HYDE

Artists: Penko Gelev
Sotir Gelev

Published by S SCRIBO
The Salariya Book Company Ltd
25 Marlborough Place, Brighton BN1 1UB
www.salariya.com

PB ISBN: 978-1-912006-01-4

SALARIYA
SCRIBO BOOK HOUSE SCRIBBLERS

1 3 5 7 9 8 6 4 2

A CIP catalogue record for this book is available
from the British Library.

Printed and bound in China.

Printed on paper from sustainable forest.

Visit
www.salariya.com
for our online catalogue and
free fun stuff.

Picture credits:
p. 43 World History Archive/TopFoto
pp. 45, 47 Topham Picturepoint/TopFoto
Every effort has been made to trace copyright holders. The Salariya Book Company apologizes for
any omissions and would be pleased, in such cases, to add an acknowledgment in future editions.

DR. JEKYLL AND MR. HYDE

ROBERT LOUIS STEVENSON

a SALARIYA *imprint*

Illustrated by

Penko Gelev

Retold by

Fiona Macdonald

Series created and designed by

David Salariya

All at once, I saw two figures: one a little man who was stumping along eastward at a good walk, and the other a girl of maybe eight or ten who was running as hard as she was able down a cross street. Well, sir, the two ran into one another naturally enough at the corner; and then came the horrible part of the thing; for the man trampled calmly over the child's body and left her screaming on the ground.

(see page 8)

CHARACTERS

Mr. Gabriel Utterson, lawyer

Mr. Richard Enfield, businessman

Dr. Henry Jekyll,
medical doctor

The mysterious
Mr. Edward Hyde

Dr. Hastie Lanyon,
scientist

Mr. Guest,
Chief Clerk to Mr. Utterson

Poole, Butler to Dr. Jekyll

A young girl

Sir Danvers Carew,
Member of Parliament

A young woman servant

Police Inspector Newcomen

Mr. Hyde's housekeeper

OLD FRIENDS

London, England, 1886

These excursions[1] are the chief jewel of each week!

Mr. Gabriel Utterson is a lawyer. He lives alone and leads a quiet life. To strangers he seems solemn and dull, but his friends respect and trust him. He is wise and understanding, and has a kind heart.

Mr. Utterson works hard from Monday to Saturday. But on Sundays he goes for long walks with his cousin, the wealthy, lively businessman Mr. Richard Enfield. Although they are so different, they have been great friends since childhood.

A small, quiet street in London

Did you ever remark[2] that door?

It is connected in my mind with a very odd story.

Indeed? And what was that?

Often they walk in silence, but today Mr. Enfield has a tale to tell.

1. excursions: journeys for pleasure.
2. remark: notice.

7

A STRANGE STORY

Mr. Enfield begins his tale:

I begin to long for the sight of a policeman.

It was very late one night. Mr. Enfield was walking home through dark, silent streets. The whole city seemed deserted. Was nobody else awake?

Suddenly two figures appeared at a street corner.

Approaching from different directions, they could not see one another.

They collided… the girl fell… the man trampled over her… and calmly walked away!

Gasp!

Owww!

Aaargh!

Halloa![1]

The child is not much the worse.

Outraged by what he had seen, Enfield chased the attacker. He soon caught him, but the man seemed completely unconcerned by what he had done.

An angry crowd gathered around the terrified girl. She was badly shaken, but still breathing. A doctor arrived, and said that she'd survive. Even the doctor looked angry enough to kill the man.

1. Halloa: a call used by huntsmen when chasing a fox.

We will make such a scandal as to make your name stink!

Name your price!

Together, Enfield and the doctor confronted the attacker: They threatened to disgrace him unless he offered money to the poor girl's family.

Sullen and sneering, the attacker agreed to pay. He was not sorry—he only wanted to avoid bad publicity.

Next, the attacker led them to a shabby door in an old outhouse, opened it, then disappeared inside. Was this a trick? Had he escaped them?

Set your mind at rest.

The whole business looks apocryphal.[3]

I will cash the check myself.

It was the same door that the two friends are looking at now!

The attacker returned with a check[1] for 100 pounds.[2] How could the stranger have got hold of this massive sum? Was the check forged, or stolen?

The attacker said he would prove that the check was not a forgery. He would wait with Mr. Enfield until the bank was open. Then they would see!

The check is genuine.

As he had promised, the attacker walked to the bank with Mr. Enfield, the doctor, and the injured girl's father.

Together, they handed the check to a bank clerk. He looked at it very carefully, and examined the signature.

As Mr. Utterson listens to this story, he shakes his head and frowns. What's worrying him?

1. check: a printed form giving one person permission to take money out of another person's bank account. It is only valid if it has been signed by the account holder.
2. 100 pounds: worth about 5,000 pounds or 10,000 U.S. dollars today.
3. apocryphal: not true.

BLACKMAIL?

Tut-tut!

I see you feel as I do. Yes, it's a bad story.

As the friends continue their walk, Mr. Enfield has more to say. The attacker was clearly evil, but the signature on the check belonged to a well-known and respected man, famous for doing good.

Blackmail!

Paying through the nose![1]

Why did this good man sign a check for the little girl's attacker? Mr. Enfield can think of only one explanation, and it is a sinister one…

Mr. Enfield supposes that the attacker knows some foolish, shameful secret from the good man's past. Now he's forcing the good man to give him money to keep that secret hidden.

Though even that, you know, is far from explaining all…

And you never asked about the place with the door?

I did not like to.

Mr. Utterson wants to know more. Does the good man live in the old outhouse with the shabby door? That's not very likely! Mr. Enfield agrees. In fact, he's discovered that the good man lives in a quiet, respectable square.[2]

1. Paying through the nose: being forced to pay too much.
2. square: a group of fine houses built around a private garden.

A very good rule, too.

It seems scarcely a house.

But Mr. Enfield has made a rule for himself: never ask questions! You never know what answers you might find. Old, bitter quarrels might be started up again, or forgotten sins made public.

Yes, I think it is.

As the friends walk on, Enfield describes the building with the door. It's not a proper house, but it has a room with three big windows, and a chimney that's often smoking. So someone must use it!

There is something wrong with his appearance. I never saw a man I so disliked, and yet I scarce know why.

I can't describe him.

It was a man by the name of Hyde.

Mr. Utterson frowns, then suddenly asks the attacker's name, and what he looked like. To Enfield's astonishment, Mr. Utterson seems to recognize the man's name. How can this be?

I do not ask you the name of the other party,[1] because I know it already!

1. the other party: the man who signed the check.

THE MYSTERY OF THE WILL

Later that evening

Mr. Utterson finishes his simple, solitary meal and goes to his office. He opens the safe where he keeps important papers, and takes out just one document.

It's a will,[1] made some time ago by one of his oldest friends.

Madness!

Mr. Utterson remembers protesting when his good friend Dr. Jekyll asked him to prepare the will. In fact, he refused to write it. Dr. Jekyll had to write it himself.

"All my possessions are to pass into the hands of my friend Edward Hyde."

Mr. Utterson has kept the will safe, but every time he sees it he feels anxious and unhappy.

A fiend! It was already bad enough when the name was but a name.[2]

1. will: a legal document giving instructions for passing on a person's money and possessions after their death.
2. "when the name was but a name": when I knew nothing about Hyde except his name.

I thought it was madness...

...now I begin to fear it is disgrace!

Mr. Utterson needs advice—urgently.

He goes to see his friend, the doctor and scientist Hastie Lanyon. Dr. Lanyon went to school with Mr. Utterson and Dr. Jekyll. Surely he'll know what to do?

You and I must be the two oldest friends that Henry Jekyll has?

He began to go wrong, wrong in mind... Such unscientific balderdash![1]

But Lanyon and Jekyll have quarrelled over a question of science. They have not spoken for more than ten years.

Did you ever come across Hyde?

No. Never heard of him.

1. balderdash: nonsense.

Hardly Human!

Back home, Mr. Utterson cannot sleep. All the strange things he's seen and heard come back to him like nightmares...

...the empty, echoing streets...

...the attacker stomping along...

...the little girl, all alone...

...the crushing attack...

...the girl's scream!

He imagines the attacker creeping up on Dr. Jekyll.

He gets closer and closer...

...looms larger and larger...

...and seems to dissolve before Utterson's eyes!

At last, as dawn breaks, Mr. Utterson falls asleep, troubled and exhausted.

14

Later that morning

Morning

Noon

Night

Mr. Utterson decides that he must track down Mr. Hyde and discover what kind of person he really is. Then, perhaps, he'll understand why Henry Jekyll is so generous to him. Utterson waits all day by the mysterious door.

At last his patience is rewarded. A small, unpleasant-looking man approaches and unlocks the shabby door.

Mr. Hyde, I think?

That is my name. What do you want?

Will you let me see your face?

Now I shall know you again. It may be useful.

It is well we have met; and you should have my address.

The man seems hardly human!

O Jekyll, if ever I read Satan's[1] signature upon a face, it is on that of your new friend!

Quick as a flash, Hyde opens the door, steps inside, and slams it shut behind him. Alone in the street, Mr. Utterson stands shocked and shaking. He, too, has seen something devilish and disgusting inside Mr. Hyde.

1. Satan's: the Devil's.

A VISIT TO DR. JEKYLL

Utterson does not go home. Instead, he goes to the square of handsome old houses where Dr. Jekyll lives. Although it's late, the lamps are still burning brightly. Mr. Utterson knocks at the front door. Poole, the butler, lets him in.

As he waits by the fire, Mr. Utterson suddenly feels a sense of menace in Dr. Jekyll's comfortable house.

As Mr. Utterson leaves, he asks Poole whether he has ever seen Mr. Hyde. Yes, he has—and he adds some startling information.

Two weeks later, Dr. Jekyll invites some old friends to his home.

I have been wanting to speak to you. You know that will of yours?

Mr. Utterson is the last to leave.

An excellent fellow, but hidebound,[1] ignorant!

You know I never approved of it. I have been learning something of young Hyde.

Dr. Jekyll looks annoyed. The will clearly worries him. He tries to change the subject: he talks about their friend Dr. Hastie Lanyon.

But Mr. Utterson is determined to help his friend Jekyll if he can. So he continues to talk about the will.

Dr. Jekyll turns deathly pale.

You do not understand. My position is very strange.

Help Hyde for my sake, when I am no longer here!

Dr. Jekyll says he is sorry, but he cannot change the will. He won't explain why. But he declares that Hyde is not as bad as Utterson fears, and promises that he can get rid of Hyde any time he chooses. Then he makes an urgent plea.

Well... I promise!

Reluctantly, Mr. Utterson agrees, but he is puzzled—and fearful. What can these desperate words mean? What terrible future lies ahead for Dr. Jekyll and the mysterious Mr. Hyde?

1. hidebound: not interested in new ideas.

A Witness to Murder

One year later

It's a fine night. The lane by the river is peaceful.

A servant girl gazes dreamily out of her window.

She sees two men: one old and dignified, the other younger and very short.

The two men meet.

The servant does not recognize the old man, but he is handsome, well-dressed, and charming. He bows to the young man, and speaks to him politely.

The young man is that horrid Mr. Hyde! He once visited her master's house, where he was rude and surly.

Gasp!

Without warning, Hyde attacks the older man.

THWACK!

CRUNCH!

Oh!

The servant faints with horror.

As soon as she revives, she hurries to call the police. They find the old man, crushed and bleeding in the gutter. Is he still breathing? No, he's dead! Hyde has murdered him. In his pocket, the police find a letter addressed to Utterson.

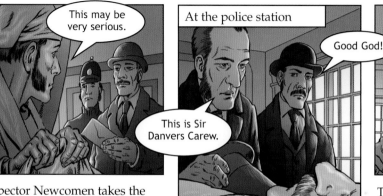

This may be very serious.

At the police station

This is Sir Danvers Carew.

Good God!

Inspector Newcomen takes the letter to Mr. Utterson straight away. He dresses quickly and goes with the police to identify the body.

The police have found half of the murder weapon—Dr. Jekyll's walking stick! Hyde must have stolen it.

He was in very late. He is often absent.

Ah! He is in trouble!

Utterson takes the police to the address that Hyde gave him. They search Hyde's rooms and question his housekeeper. Hyde is not there—but they find the other half of the broken walking stick.

WHO EXACTLY IS MR. HYDE?

Later the same day

Mr. Utterson calls at Dr. Jekyll's house. Poole, the butler, leads him to the Doctor's private laboratory in an old outbuilding behind the house. Mr. Utterson has never been here before. It is dingy, dusty, and full of mysterious flasks and test tubes. Dr. Jekyll is huddled by the fire, looking very ill.

You have heard the news?[1]

They were crying[2] it in the street.

I swear to God I will never set eyes on him again. It is all at an end. He will never more be heard of.

I want to know...

You have not been mad enough to hide this fellow?

As a lawyer, Utterson has a duty to help catch the murderer. But he is also very loyal to his fine old friend, Dr. Jekyll. He questions the Doctor carefully. Has he been sheltering the murderous Mr. Hyde?

1. the news: the murder of Sir Danvers Carew.
2. crying: shouting. Newspaper sellers used to shout out the headlines in the street.

Mr. Utterson is very worried by Dr. Jekyll's wild, feverish way of talking. He warns him, sternly, never to see Hyde again.

Dr. Jekyll promises, over and over again. Then he hands Mr. Utterson a letter that has just arrived. Should he show it to the police? It is signed "Edward Hyde."

The letter thanks Jekyll for his help in the past, and says that Hyde has found a sure way to escape—and stay away.

Dr. Jekyll still does not want to talk about the will, but he finally admits that Hyde forced him to make it.

Back in his office, Mr. Utterson takes a closer look at the letter. He shows it to Mr. Guest, his head clerk, who is an expert on handwriting.

A servant brings a note from Dr. Jekyll. It's nothing urgent, just an invitation to dinner later in the week.

Guest asks to look at the invitation. He places it next to the letter, and compares them. Mr. Utterson can hardly bear to think what Guest might discover!

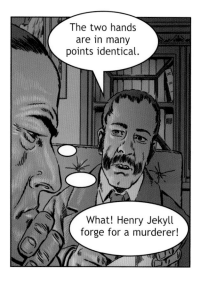

1. circulars: advertisements; "junk mail."
2. singular resemblance: unusual likeness.

HYDE HAS VANISHED!

All London is gripped by news of the shocking crime. A huge reward is offered for information.

So callous[1] and violent!

Thousands of pounds in reward!

But Hyde is nowhere to be found. His disappearance has led to one good thing: Dr. Jekyll seems much happier, and is busy helping the sick and poor.

Now Dr. Jekyll sees much more of his friends. He is kindly, lively, welcoming. He has even forgotten his old quarrel with Dr. Hastie Lanyon. The two of them dine with Mr. Utterson. It's just like the good old days!

A few days later

The Doctor is confined to the house.[2]

Utterson is told that Dr. Jekyll is not well.

A week later

The Doctor is seeing no one.

I have had a shock, and I shall never recover.

Even worse, when Mr. Utterson calls on Dr. Lanyon to ask his advice, he finds that Lanyon is dying!

---

1. callous: cruel and uncaring.
2. confined to the house: having to stay indoors because he is ill.

It is a question of weeks.

Jekyll is ill too. Have you seen him?

What dreadful thing can have happened to Mr. Utterson's two old friends?

I wish to see or hear no more of Doctor Jekyll.

Can't I do anything?

Nothing.

As soon as he gets home, Mr. Utterson sits down and writes to Dr. Jekyll. He must see him! He has to know: why have the two doctors quarrelled so disastrously? And why won't Dr. Jekyll see anyone?

"If I am the chief of sinners, I am the chief of sufferers also."

At last Jekyll replies.

"I have brought on myself a punishment and a danger that I cannot name."

Dr. Jekyll's reply is baffling. Mr. Utterson is still puzzling over it when he hears the dreadful news that Dr. Lanyon has died. Mr. Utterson mourns the passing of his trusty old friend.

THE LABORATORY WINDOW

> I have buried one friend today; what if this letter should cost me another?

Soon after Dr. Lanyon fell ill, he gave Mr. Utterson a sealed envelope. Fearful of what it might reveal, Mr. Utterson now opens it.

Inside is an envelope marked, "Not to be opened till the death or disappearance of Dr. Henry Jekyll." Utterson puts it away and hurries to Jekyll's house.

> But again Dr. Jekyll is seeing no one.

> The Doctor is out of spirits.[1] It seems as if he has something on his mind.

Utterson and Enfield still enjoy their Sunday walks.

> Well, we shall never see more of Mr. Hyde.

> I hope not. Did I ever tell you that I once saw him?

They happen to walk past the shabby door.

> This is a back way to Dr. Jekyll's!

Mr. Enfield has finally realized where this door leads to.

> To tell you the truth, I am uneasy about poor Jekyll.

Mr. Utterson already knew this, but had not told anyone. Now he thinks it is time to share his worries.

He suggests that they visit Dr. Jekyll. Some cheerful, friendly conversation, perhaps even a walk in the fresh air, might do him good.

> Jekyll! I trust you are better.

Dr. Jekyll is seated at one of the laboratory windows.

1. out of spirits: depressed.

Utterson and Enfield look on, appalled.
They cannot help poor Dr. Jekyll. Slowly,
grimly, they continue their walk in silence.
At last Mr. Utterson speaks. His words
reveal his desperation.

2. low: ill and depressed.

DR. JEKYLL MURDERED?

"Bless me, Poole, what brings you here? Is the Doctor ill?"

One evening, not long afterward

Mr. Utterson is astonished to receive a visit from Poole, Dr. Jekyll's butler. Poole looks worried and flustered. What can the matter be?

"I can bear it no more! I think there's been foul play.[1]"

Dr. Jekyll has been behaving very strangely. He's been shut up in his laboratory for over a week. Poole is at his wits' end.

The two men hurry to Dr. Jekyll's house.

"God grant there be nothing wrong!"

They find the servants almost hysterical.

"They're all afraid."

Poole and Utterson head for Dr. Jekyll's laboratory.

"Come as gently as you can."

"If he was to ask you in, don't go!"

"Mr. Utterson, sir, asking to see you."

KNOCK, KNOCK!

1. foul play: murder.

Tell him I cannot see anyone!

Was that my master's voice?

It seems much changed.

Changed? Well, yes, I think so!

At first there is silence. But then Poole and Mr. Utterson hear a faint, feeble voice. It seems to be coming from some far corner of the laboratory.

Mr. Utterson doesn't recognize the voice. Can that really be his old friend, Henry Jekyll? If so, something's wrong!

This is rather a wild tale.

This drug is wanted bitter bad, sir.

Poole thinks that Dr. Jekyll was murdered about a week ago. The murderer is still there, gloating over Dr. Jekyll's body and pretending to be him!

Mr. Utterson is doubtful. Why would a murderer risk staying so close to the scene of the crime? Poole thinks he knows why.

Every day the impostor sends Poole out to buy rare chemicals. He is obviously desperate for some mysterious potion.

I've seen him!

Well?

Sir, that thing was not my master!

Strangely, the notes ordering chemicals have all been in Dr. Jekyll's handwriting. But once Poole glimpsed a sinister shape scurrying into the laboratory.

THE END OF MR. HYDE

I consider it my duty to break in that door.

Once I heard weeping like a lost soul.

Jekyll, I demand to see you!

Mr. Utterson must find out what is going on in the laboratory. He asks Poole and the other servants to help him. They are all terrified, but they will do their best.

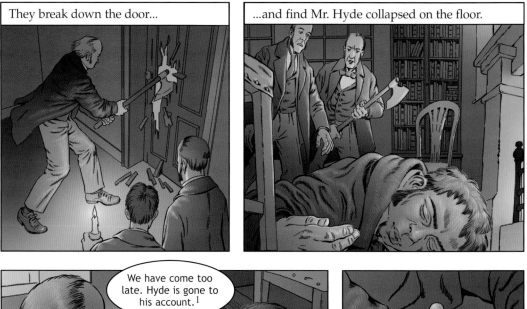

They break down the door...

...and find Mr. Hyde collapsed on the floor.

We have come too late. Hyde is gone to his account.[1]

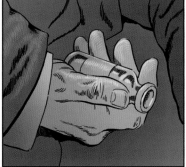

Clutched in Hyde's lifeless hand is a glass bottle. It smells strongly of bitter almonds—it is cyanide, a swift-acting, deadly poison.

1. gone to his account: gone to be judged by God—that is, dead.

He must be buried here.

But where is Jekyll's body?

Or he may have fled.

That is the same drug I was always bringing him.

They find chemicals scattered on the workbench...

...and a holy book— vandalized!

Blasphemies![1]

Then they notice a full-length mirror. Why is that in the laboratory?

This mirror has seen some strange things, sir!

What could Jekyll want with it?

On the desk is an envelope addressed to Mr. Utterson.

Mr. Utterson

My head is spinning!

It is a new will, in Dr. Jekyll's handwriting. He now leaves all his money *not* to Mr. Hyde, but to Mr. Gabriel Utterson! There is also a letter with today's date.

He was alive and here this day! O, we must be careful!

Utterson reads it gloomily: "When this shall fall into your hands, I shall have disappeared... Your unworthy and unhappy friend, Henry Jekyll."

1. Blasphemies: offensive, unholy words or sayings.

29

DR. LANYON'S STORY

A few months earlier

A registered[1] envelope?

Back home in his office, Mr. Utterson puts Dr. Jekyll's documents to one side. Now that Jekyll has vanished, it is time to read the sealed letter from the late Dr. Lanyon. The letter has a terrible tale to tell...

Dr. Lanyon—then strong and healthy—was busy in his study when a servant brought him an urgent message that had just arrived.

"You are one of my oldest friends. If you fail[2] me tonight, I am lost!"

It was from Dr. Jekyll. Dr. Lanyon was very surprised. It contained detailed instructions.

"I want you to take a cab and drive straight to my house."

"Poole has his orders."

"You will find him waiting with a locksmith."

"Open the glazed press."[3]

"Draw[4] out the fourth drawer from the top..."

1. registered: sent by special secure mail.
2. fail: refuse to help.
3. glazed press: big cupboard with glass doors.
4. Draw: pull.

30

"...with all its contents: some powders, a phial,[1] and a book."

Dr. Lanyon followed the instructions carefully and carried the drawer back to his house.

He examined the contents, then sat waiting...

...for a midnight knock at the door.

KNOCK, KNOCK!

He let the caller in...

Did you come from Dr. Jekyll?

and led him to the study.

Have you got it? Have you got it?

Aaaaahhhhh!

The repulsive caller—it was Hyde, although Dr. Lanyon did not know him—was oddly dressed in elegant clothes that were far too big for him. He was obviously desperate to have the things in the drawer.

1. phial: small glass bottle for drugs or chemicals.

THE TRANSFORMATION

The repulsive man asked Dr. Lanyon for a measuring glass, then took some white powder and red liquid from the drawer and mixed them together.

The mixture fizzed and bubbled.

It turned deep purple…

…and finally bright green.

Smiling broadly, Hyde turned to Dr. Lanyon.

And now new knowledge and power shall be laid open to you!

Sir, you speak enigmas. [1]

Behold!

AAARGH!

Hyde gasped, staggered, and clung to the table, staring with wild eyes, panting, open-mouthed.

1. enigmas: riddles, mysteries.

Then his face seemed to swell...

the features seemed to melt and change...

...and there before Dr. Lanyon stood Henry Jekyll!

O God! O God!

Lanyon sat shaking, sickened and appalled, as Dr. Jekyll began to explain. Every word seemed like a deadly blow, destroying his mind, his soul, his reason! His whole world collapsed around him, leaving only horror, horror, horror.

My life is shaken to its roots. I must die!

"I saw what I saw, I heard what I heard, and my soul sickened at it."

Dr. Lanyon could not bring himself to write down all the foul secrets Dr. Jekyll told him. But he did record, in his letter to Mr. Utterson, that Dr. Jekyll confessed to being Edward Hyde—the murderer of Sir Danvers Carew!

Dr. Jekyll Tells his Story

The letter tells Henry Jekyll's life story.

Mr. Utterson can hardly believe what Dr. Lanyon has written. How can Jekyll and Hyde be the same person?

With trembling hands he opens the sealed letter that he found beside Dr. Jekyll's new will. Will this explain the mystery? Frantically, he reads on…

"I was born to a rich, respectable family. As a young man I was intelligent, hardworking, keen to win praise and fame. A bright future lay ahead for me."

"Alone at night and at crowded scientific lectures, I studied hard to cure sickness and ease suffering."

"My only fault was a light-hearted love of pleasure. I enjoyed having fun! I never broke the law or harmed anyone."

Man is not truly one, but truly two!

It is the curse of mankind!

"But, even so, I felt deeply ashamed. I was proud, and wanted to appear pure and noble. So I kept my pleasures secret, and began to feel extremely guilty about them."

"I came to think that there were two sides to human nature: the good and the evil."

"The good side and the bad side are tightly joined together. If only they could be parted!"

Eurghh!

"One day, in my laboratory, I created an exciting—and dangerous—new potion. It was designed to separate the good and bad parts in each person."

"I drank it in one gulp! Terrible pains followed: a grinding in my bones, dreadful sickness, and nameless terror."

I feel younger, lighter, happier!

"Soon the pain passed, and delightful new sensations gripped me. But I found I was also much smaller..."

and most unpleasant to look at! My whole face and body had become cruel and ugly, just like the evil soul within."

Welcome! This, too, is myself!

"As I gazed into the mirror, I realized that I had become two people: good Dr. Jekyll, and shameless Mr. Hyde. Jekyll had his medical training to guide his thoughts and actions. But Hyde was pure evil—and completely out of control!"

"Day was fast approaching. I dared not be seen in my changed shape. So I mixed some more of the potion, drank it quickly, and turned back into solemn, serious Dr. Henry Jekyll."

LEADING A DOUBLE LIFE

Dr. Jekyll's life story continues...

"Before long, a terrible plan took shape in my mind. Whenever I wanted to have fun without feeling guilty...

...I just had to drink a glass of the potion and turn into Mr. Hyde. He could do what he liked, without guilt or regret."

"As Mr. Hyde, I rented rooms in a part of London famous for its wild nightlife. Many criminals lived there, too. The landlady asked no questions!"

"As Dr. Jekyll, I told all my servants to welcome and obey Mr. Hyde if ever he came to my home. I tested them once or twice, by appearing as Mr. Hyde."

"Next I came to see you, Utterson, my lawyer friend, and made the will that you hated."

"Now Hyde was free to do whatever he liked— and no one would ever suspect Henry Jekyll!"

"Before, my pleasures had been silly but harmless. Now they became cruel and vicious. I was savage and dangerous, like a wild beast."

"I delighted in violence and suffering."

"I trampled down innocent victims, just for the cold thrill it gave me!"

"But one morning—horror!"

"I had gone to bed Henry Jekyll..."

and awakened Edward Hyde!"

My drugs!

"My blood turned to ice."

"As quickly and quietly as I could, I crept to my laboratory and mixed myself a strong dose of the potion."

"It worked! Within minutes, I was dressed and ready to go downstairs and eat breakfast as my other self, Dr. Jekyll."

I have to choose!

"That night was a warning to me! I was losing hold of my good self and being taken over entirely by my bad self. What if Dr. Jekyll turned into the monstrous Mr. Hyde forever?"

"Of course, I chose to be Jekyll. For two whole months I said my prayers, did good deeds, and lived a quiet, hardworking life. But I missed the freedom, the pleasure—and the dangerous excitement—of Hyde's evil adventures."

TRAPPED!

My devil has been long caged, now he comes out roaring!

"The longing grew so great that I could not resist it. One fateful night I swallowed another dose of the potion. Immediately, I was transformed."

"You know how I met and attacked Sir Danvers Carew, then hurried away to my lodgings."

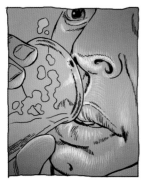

Aaargh!

"There, I quickly drank some of the potion to escape from Hyde's bloodstained body."

"With enormous relief, I changed back into respectable Dr. Jekyll. I was safe! The police could never find me."

"But one fine day I went for a stroll in the park. Still Dr. Jekyll, I sat down to enjoy the sunshine. But a shudder came over me, then sickness, then grinding pain…"

My drugs— how am I to reach them?

…and I found myself turning into Mr. Hyde! Now I was a hateful murderer, hunted throughout London. If they caught me, I'd be hanged—and my potion was at Dr. Jekyll's home."

"I hid in a hotel room until it was dark, and sent urgent letters to Poole and Dr. Lanyon."

"At midnight I called at Dr. Lanyon's house. He had kindly fetched my potion in the drawer, so I was safe again."

"But not for long!"

"The potion seemed to be losing its strength."

"Again and again…

…I turned into Mr. Hyde!"

The horror of being Hyde!

"It was a nightmare!"

He! he!

But I find it in my heart to pity him.

"As I grew weaker, Hyde became stronger. Helplessly, I changed into his horrid shape several times a day."

"Hyde sensed my fear and tormented me, smashing and burning my most treasured possessions."

"He was primitive, savage, less than human. He was dust and slime, without feelings. He belonged to an earlier, undeveloped era in mankind's history— but he was also alive in me!"

This is the true hour of my death.

I bring the life of that unhappy Henry Jekyll to an end!

"Now I have run out of chemicals to mix my potion. I keep sending Poole for more, but they do not work. My first mixture must have had some impurity in it which gave it its special power."

"So I am trapped. Soon I will be transformed into Hyde yet again, and I have no potion left to turn me back again. Will Hyde be caught and hanged for murder, or will he have the courage to end this misery by killing himself?"

THE END

39

ROBERT LOUIS STEVENSON (1850–1894)

Robert Louis Stevenson was born in Edinburgh, Scotland, on November 13, 1850. He was the only son of Thomas Stevenson and his wife Margaret Isabella Balfour. Both families were wealthy, well educated, and very respectable. Robert's mother suffered from tuberculosis, and it is unclear whether she passed the disease on to him, or whether he suffered from another lung disorder. He was often too sick to attend school, and so lay in bed, reading or composing poems and stories of his own.

Robert Louis Stevenson, from an image held at Bishop Museum, Hawaii.

UNIVERSITY

Aged 17, he enrolled at Edinburgh University. His father wanted him to study engineering, but Robert wanted to be a writer. As a compromise he studied law, but spent all his spare time writing. During vacations he traveled to France to meet other young artists and writers. He was often sick, but always lively-minded, unconventional, and determined.

MARRIAGE

Robert qualified as a lawyer in 1875, but never worked in the profession. His first book, about a canoeing expedition in France, was published in 1878, and he spent the rest of his life as a writer. In France, Robert also met the woman who would later become his wife: Fanny Van de Grift Osbourne, an American. They were a strange couple, but passionately in love. She was everything he was not: loud, healthy,

and vibrant. Robert's family was not happy, because Fanny was 11 years older than Robert, and was already married. In 1880, after Fanny's divorce, Robert traveled to America to marry her. Robert's family was appalled, but the couple was happy together.

FIRST NOVEL

In 1881 Robert and Fanny traveled to Scotland with Fanny's son, Lloyd Osbourne. They made peace with Robert's family, and visited the Highlands with them. But the cold and rain worsened Robert's health, so they soon left in search of milder weather. They went to Switzerland, France, and the south of England, then back to America. All the time, Robert wrote—he produced travel books, poems, and short stories.

Then, in 1883, he published his first long novel. Its title was *Treasure Island*. During the next six years Robert wrote four more novels. These included his most famous work, *The Strange Case of Dr. Jekyll and Mr. Hyde*. This brilliant fantasy thriller was an instant bestseller and made him famous throughout Britain and America.

DETERIORATING HEALTH

By 1887 Robert's health was getting worse, so he and Fanny returned to America with his mother (his father had died). Then, with Fanny's children, they set sail across the Pacific Ocean.

SAMOA

After a long voyage they settled on the island of Samoa. They built a house and made friends with the islanders, who called Robert "Tusitala" ("Teller of Tales"). Robert was fascinated by the islands and their rich heritage of songs and stories. He collected information for a huge history of the Pacific, campaigned to stop Europeans ill-treating local people, and wrote poems and stories about the island. Robert also wrote novels set in faraway Scotland. The last of these, *Weir of Hermiston*, which he never finished, was probably his best piece of writing.

Sadly, even the warm Pacific climate could not cure Robert's illness, and he died suddenly on December 3, 1894 at just 44 years old. He was buried on the top of Mount Vaea, above his home in Samoa, and lines from his own poem "Requiem" were carved on his tomb:

Under the wide and starry sky,
Dig the grave and let me lie.
Glad did I live and gladly die,
And I laid me down with a will.

OTHER BOOKS WRITTEN BY

ROBERT LOUIS STEVENSON

1878	*An Inland Voyage*
1879	*Travels with a Donkey in the Cévennes*
1883	*Treasure Island*
1884	*The Silverado Squatters*
1885	*A Child's Garden of Verses*
1885	*The Body Snatcher*
1886	*Kidnapped*

1886	*The Strange Case of Dr. Jekyll and Mr. Hyde*
1888	*The Black Arrow*
1889	*The Master of Ballantrae*
1892	*The Wrong Box*
1896	*Weir of Hermiston*

(published posthumously; Stevenson was working on this the day he died.)

obert Louis Stevenson wrote *The Strange Case of Dr. Jekyll and Mr. Hyde* for an urgent reason—to make money. He had been working as a professional writer since he was 21 years old, and his books had won praise. But in 1885, aged 35, he still relied on gifts of money from his father to survive—and, as well as himself, he had a wife and a lively young stepson to support. So he was delighted when, in 1885, his editor at Longman, the powerful London publishing company, asked him to write a "shilling shocker" (a cheap, exciting story) to sell at Christmas.

CHRISTMAS HORROR

The Christmas holiday was a time when many 19th-century readers liked to relax by their cozy family firesides with an easy-to-read story that would give them a safe-but-shocking thrill. Publishing horror tales at Christmas had been a favorite British tradition ever since the great popular success of Charles Dickens' ghost story *A Christmas Carol*, which first appeared in 1843. Long before then, the British reading public had enjoyed full-length horror novels such as *The Castle of Otranto* by Horace Walpole (published on Christmas Eve, 1764), *The Mysteries of Udolpho* by Anne Radcliffe (1794), and *Frankenstein* by Mary Shelley (1818). Stevenson himself had published earlier "shilling shockers" for Christmas: *The Body Snatcher* in 1884 and *Olalla* (a vampire tale) in 1885.

FICTION FOR THE MASSES

By the time Stevenson's Christmas stories were published, new printing and picture technology, such as rotary presses and steel engraving, made it quick, cheap, and easy to print reading matter in large quantities. This meant that books were now more affordable in Britain than they had ever been before. More British people were able to read, too. Since the 1870s, primary education had been compulsory. This meant that ordinary people, as well as the wealthy, were taught to read and write, and a new mass market for cheap books, illustrated magazines, and newspapers was created.

A PUBLISHING SENSATION

In fact, there were so many books planned for Christmas 1885 that the publishers held back *Jekyll and Hyde* until early the next year, 1886. It became an overnight sensation, selling 40,000 copies in just six weeks. Even Queen Victoria herself was said to have read it eagerly. Since then, Stevenson's "shilling shocker" has been enjoyed, in different formats, by millions of people all around the world. The names of his two main characters, Jekyll and Hyde, have passed into the English language as a shorthand way of describing anyone or anything that has a double nature, with good and bad sides.

Stevenson claimed that the idea for the story came to him in a dream. His wife Fanny woke him up before the dream was over, fearing that he was being tormented by a terrifying nightmare. Angrily, Stevenson complained, "I was dreaming a fine bogie [monster] tale." The original title was *Strange Case of Dr. Jekyll and Mr. Hyde*—without a "the" at the beginning—which makes it sound like a sensational newspaper headline.

FACT AND FICTION

What inspired Stevenson to write *Jekyll and Hyde*? Years after Stevenson died, his family still claimed that the story came to him in a dream. This may be true, but scholars have also suggested that real-life events and discoveries may have excited Stevenson's imagination. Many of these were connected with Edinburgh, the capital city of Scotland. Stevenson spent the first half of his life there, and studied at Edinburgh's famous university, which had (and still has) a world-class medical school. Stevenson's family were respectable Edinburgh citizens, but he rebelled against the city's strict—and sometimes hypocritical—way of life.

Other ideas that may have inspired Stevenson included the new theory of evolution (the word was first used in 1852) and controversial theories about criminal behavior. The theory of evolution suggested that humanity had gradually evolved (changed) from primitive, unthinking, uncontrolled animals to thoughtful, self-controlled people—an idea that many people found shocking and ridiculous. Some 19th-century scientists believed that traces of savage "primitive" human nature still survived inside the most "civilized" humans.

Other scientists looked for medical reasons to explain why people behaved badly. They suggested that some habits or pleasures weakened a human's sense of good and bad. Others thought that criminals were a "lower," less developed type of humanity and could be recognized by physical features such as the shape of the skull.

Mr. Hyde unlocks the mysterious door. A drawing by Edmund J. Sullivan published in 1928.

DR. JEKYLL'S NAME

Although Jekyll is an unusual name, it is a real English surname. The most famous Jekyll in real life was the gardener Gertrude Jekyll (1843–1932); Stevenson was a friend of her brother, the Reverend Walter Jekyll. The name should really be pronounced "JEE-kill," not "JECK-ill."

1765–1850
The polite, clean, elegant New Town district of Edinburgh is built for rich, respectable people to live in (Stevenson's family moved there in 1857). Poor people had to go on living in Edinburgh's rough, dirty, unhealthy Old Town.

1788
Execution of William "Deacon" Brodie, an Edinburgh woodworker who behaved very well during the day but committed robberies at night. As a young man, Stevenson heard many stories about Brodie's double life. Some Edinburgh people claimed that Brodie had survived and still lurked about the city.

1793
Death of Dr. John Hunter, a famous Edinburgh surgeon and pioneer of anatomy (the study of how the body works). Hunter kept a famous collection of preserved body parts, which Stevenson visited.

1822
British writer Thomas de Quincey publishes *Confessions of an English Opium Eater*, about his damaging drug addiction.

1824
Scottish writer James Hogg publishes a horror story, *Memoirs and Confessions of a Justified Sinner*. Set in and around Edinburgh, it tells a tale from two different points of view: those of a calm, sensible Editor, and a wild, perhaps mad, Sinner. Hogg also includes a religious theme that Stevenson knew well: the strict Christian (Protestant) teaching that some people are damned, whatever they do, and will end their lives in Hell.

1829
Execution of William Burke, an Irish laborer who lived in Edinburgh. With his partner in crime, William Hare, Burke killed between 16 and 30 Edinburgh citizens. He sold the bodies to a respectable Edinburgh doctor, Robert Knox, who cut them up to study them. Hare was pardoned and moved to London, where he died as a beggar in 1859. Knox was never put on trial—though he probably knew how the bodies were obtained—and died, famous, in 1862.

1829
Scottish philosopher James Mill publishes *An Analysis of the Phenomena of the Human Mind*.

1835
British investigator James Pritchard publishes *A Treatise on Insanity and Other Disorders Affecting the Mind*.

1837
German-Estonian scientist Karl von Baer observes that the embryos (unborn young) of different species look similar. This leads some scholars to ask, "What makes humans develop into thinking, responsible creatures?"

1842
A way of classifying different humans according to the size and shape of their skull is suggested by Swedish scientist Anders Retzius.

1842–1847
Anesthetic (consciousness-changing) effects of certain gases discovered by American doctor Crawford Long, American dentists Horace Wells and William Morton, and British doctors John Snow and James Simpson.

1850s
Young Robert Louis Stevenson is thrilled—and scared—by stories about Thomas Weir, told by his nanny. Weir was a respectable Edinburgh man who confessed in 1670 to a double life of witchcraft, and was executed.

1852
The word "evolution" is coined by British philosopher Herbert Spencer.

1856
Remains of a prehistoric, "primitive" human (known as Neanderthal Man) are found in Germany.

1859
The Origin of Species by Means of Natural Selection is published by British scientist Charles Darwin. It introduces his theory that all living things change and develop over time.

1859
The highly-addictive drug cocaine, which alters mood and behavior, is first prepared in a laboratory by German chemist Albert Neimann.

1863
British undertaker William Banting invents the first extreme diet designed to change a person's body shape.

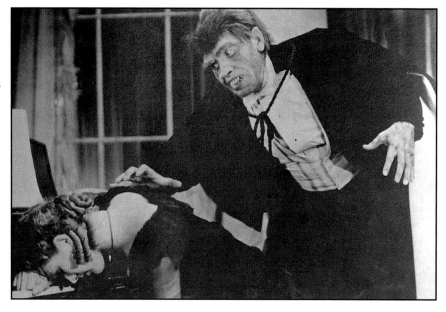

A rather over-the-top Mr. Hyde (Fredric March) claims a victim in the 1931 Paramount movie of Dr. Jekyll and Mr. Hyde.

1865
Biological laws of heredity discovered by Gregor Mendel, from Moravia (now Czech Republic). Mendel showed that physical characteristics are passed from one generation to the next. Even today, experts still debate how far human behavior is caused by heredity.

1866
Russian writer Fyodor Dostoyevsky publishes his philosophical novel *Crime and Punishment*, about a man who thinks he can commit a murder without feeling guilty, but finds that he cannot.

1866
The theory that an animal's early childhood development reveals its past evolution is published by German scientist Ernst Haeckel.

1868
Fossils of the earliest-known primitive human in Europe (known as Cro-Magnon Man) are found in France.

1869
DNA, the part of living cells that carries genes from one generation to the next, is discovered by German biochemist Friedrich Miescher.

1871
Charles Darwin publishes *The Descent of Man*. It suggests that humans evolved from apes.

1873 and 1874
British investigator Henry Maudsley publishes two books about mental illness and crime.

1879
Russian psychologist Ivan Pavlov performs experiments on dogs to investigate the causes of different kinds of behavior.

1880s
Scientists in Europe discover the bacteria (germs) that cause many serious diseases, and often deform (badly change) human bodies.

1883
The word "eugenics" is invented to describe the very controversial theory that humanity can be "improved" by careful breeding.

1886
German doctor Richard von Krafft-Ebing publishes the results of his investigations into abnormal behavior. He believes this is often caused by diseases of the mind or body.

Since 1887, the year after Stevenson's story was published, the tale of Jekyll and Hyde has inspired hundreds of stage plays, movies, and TV shows in the USA and Europe. They range from children's cartoons, such as *The Case of the Stuttering Pig* (Looney Tunes, 1937) and *Hyde and Hare* (featuring Bugs Bunny, 1955), to comedy versions like *The Nutty Professor* (1963), and a musical, *After You, Mr. Hyde* (1968). The character of Dr. Jekyll/Mr. Hyde has also starred in violent horror movies, often together with other disturbing creatures such as Frankenstein's monster.

Few movies or TV programs follow Robert Louis Stevenson's original text closely; many—like the British children's TV series *Julia Jekyll and Harriet Hyde* (BBC, 1995)—simply tell a tale of transformation brought about by drinking a magic potion. Many versions add new female characters to create a love interest. This trend began with the first stage play, *Dr. Jekyll and Mr. Hyde*, written by Thomas Russell Sullivan and produced in Boston, Mass., in 1887.

However, the following treatments of the Jekyll and Hyde story have won praise from critics as entertainments in their own right, have proved popular with audiences, or both:

1920
Dr. Jekyll and Mr. Hyde, Paramount-Artcraft, USA. A silent black-and-white movie starring John Barrymore as a spider-like Hyde. According to cinema legend, Barrymore did the transformation scene without any special make-up.

1931
Dr. Jekyll and Mr. Hyde, Paramount, USA. A silent black-and-white movie directed by Rouben Mamoulian. Now valued as a classic. Stars Fredric March as a hairy, ape-like Mr. Hyde (see page 45).

1941
Dr. Jekyll and Mr. Hyde, Paramount Studios. A "talkie," in black and white, starring celebrity actors Spencer Tracy, Lana Turner, and Ingrid Bergman. The movie is also famous for its dramatic, atmospheric music.

1955
The Strange Case of Dr. Jekyll and Mr. Hyde, CBS. Part of the TV series *Climax!* Black and white. Close to Stevenson's original story.

1959
Experiment in Evil (US title), France, directed for TV by famous filmmaker Jean Renoir. Set in Paris, starring French actor Jean-Louis Barrault.

1960
The Two Faces of Dr. Jekyll, Hammer Horror, UK. With many lurid scenes.

1968
The Strange Case of Dr. Jekyll and Mr. Hyde, CBC, USA/Canada. A TV mini-series starring Jack Palance. Nominated for an Emmy Award for Outstanding Dramatic Programs.

1971
Dr. Jekyll and Sister Hyde, EMI/Hammer, UK. In this version Dr. Jekyll is transformed into a woman.

1990
Jekyll and Hyde, London Weekend Television, UK. A two-part TV movie starring Michael Caine. Made in the great British costume-drama tradition.

1994
Mary Reilly, Tristar, USA. The Jekyll and Hyde story as seen by Dr. Jekyll's housemaid. Starring Julia Roberts and John Malkovich. With computer-generated special effects.

1995
Dr. Jekyll and Ms. Hyde, Savoy Pictures, USA. A comedy version involving strange potions and sinister plots in a chemical factory that makes perfumes.

2007
Jekyll, BBC, UK. A six-part TV series starring James Nesbitt. A continuation of Stevenson's story, set in the present day and involving a descendant of the original Dr. Jekyll.

John Barrymore (right) as Hyde in the 1920 Paramount movie.

INDEX

OTHER TITLES IN THIS SERIES:

PB ISBN: 978-1-912006-22-9

PB ISBN: 978-1-912006-02-1